THE CRYSTALS of EXISTENCE

Ephraim Nwabuko

THE CRYSTALS *of* EXISTENCE

Ephraim Nwabuko

Published by:
Eleviv Publishing Group
Centerville, OH 45458
info@elevivpublishing.com
www.elevivpublishing.com

ISBN: 978-1-952744-55-6 (PB)
        978-1-952744-65-5 (HC)
        978-1-952744-69-3 (E-book)

Printed in the United States of America

ACKNOWLEDGEMENTS

In writing this book, I was supported by many loving people, and I am thankful to them. I want to say a big thank you to my parents, who always encouraged me to write, prophesying that I would be an author early on. My appreciation also goes to my sisters for giving me ideas on what to write. And to my brother for role-playing characters and giving his thoughts on the book. Most importantly, I am grateful to God, who gave me the knowledge and strength to write this book. I hope you enjoy the story as you read.

TABLE OF CONTENTS

Since the dawn of the Earth, life has been thriving on the planet. The true essence of life on a planet is sustained by the source. On Earth, the source that sustains life are the five elemental crystals. Moon, Time, Water, Earth, and Spirit. They are called the Crystals of Existence. Each crystal wields individual power, but a planet's source of power can be its demise all the same. If some being gets hold of each of a planet's life sources, they can use it to drain all life on it.

ENCOUNTER

In a small town called Horads, there is a boy named Algar Newman. Algar and his family have extraordinary power. What makes this power special is that it is drawn from no Crystal. The Newmans have lived in this town for generations, using their powers to bring prosperity to it. Algar's abilities were far beyond the capacity of his family. But he keeps himself in check, and his power follows suit. They lived happy lives in Horads until something higher was called to them.

A black Sedan with a Cadillac entourage pulled up to Newman's home.

"United Governance! Open up!" Knocked

the officials.

Algar opened the door. He looked up and saw a tall agent of the United Governance.

"Can I help you, madam?" said Father Newman.

"I'd like a word with your son, Algar Newman."

"Might I ask why?" Algar asked.

"Algar Newman, you've been called to the United Governance National Capital. You're coming with us." The agent replied.

"The capital? But, why?" Mother Newman asked.

"Information is confidential. The President of the United Governance of America, Ben Zalkon, needs to speak with Algar urgently. It is a life and death matter."

"But why Algar? He has nothing to do with the president of the nation." Father Newman said. Algar quickly interjected.

"I'll go." He said.

"Algar, why? You don't know these people." Mother said.

"Something tells me that this is more than helping a small village. Something tells me that my power is for a higher calling."

"It's then settled. Algar Newman, you have a meeting with the president." The agent said.

UNITED GOVERNANCE NATIONAL CAPITAL

After a long journey across the nation, Algar arrived at the UGA National Capital to meet President Zalkon.

Algar expected to head straight to the Gold Citadel where the president lived, but the transportation went a different route. Algar was nervous. He knew the government had been eying his power, but he felt that this meeting would discuss something above him. Finally, Algar, the agent, and the entourage arrived on an empty plain on the outskirts of the capital.

"What are we doing here? I thought we were meeting with President Zalkon." Algar asked the agent.

"We are."
The agent pulled a remote from her pocket and pressed its central button. Suddenly, the ground began to shake as a metal entrance rose from the ground. Then the agent said, "We're here."

"Secret United Governance Secure Facility Area 1."

AITKEN BASIN, MOON

"Where is the Moon Crystal? Our star maps directed us here." said the being.

"Sire, it appears the humans have taken the

jewel and moved it to the surface of the planet."

"Where?" he asked.

"Its Earthly coordinates are 38.95,-77.1553. In an underground facility."

"Then I'll fish it out."

UGA SECURE FACILITY

"So, where are we off to now that we're in this place?" Algar asked.

"The president's chamber." The agent replied.

"His chamber? Isn't his operations in the Gold Citadel?"

"Yes. This facility holds a special treasure. That is part of the reason President Zalkon called you here. He'll explain everything shortly."

Suddenly, Algar had a bad feeling about the upcoming event. As they approached the metal doors with the United Governance of America insignia, Algar tried to soothe his mind with a question.

"Agent, I never got your name," Algar said.

"Agent Carlson. Amanda Carlson."

"It's been a pleasure meeting, Agent Carlson."

"The pleasures not done yet."

Agent Carlson types a code to open the door. Air escapes the room in a rush. Algar is edgy. Generals and high-ranking officers fill the room. At the far side stands President Zalkon.

MOON

"Algar Newman, it's an honor to meet you," Zalkon said.

"The pleasures all yours, I mean, mine, your excellency." Algar stammered.
The President chuckled.

"I assume you've met Agent Carlson beside you?"

"Yes. I have. I got the word you called me here for this meeting."

"Yes, there is a matter of the utmost importance. All life on Earth depends on it."
Algar quaked in fear. A general stepped up.

"Since the dawn of Earth, life has thrived on

the surface. Five power-filled crystals sustain and prosper life. They are as follows. Moon, Time, Water, Earth, and Spirit. The Moon Crystal was brought to the surface 52 years ago. It's been kept in this facility since."

The general pushes a button on the table. The center of the table opened, and a levitating metal cube floated up. It opened, revealing the jagged gray crystal, teeming with power. Algar looked in amazement.

"The Time Crystal is somewhere in Chengdu, the People's Republic of China. It's in possession of rogue Master Tai Fang Wu. The gem operates all machines of time, from clocks to hourglasses. It makes the world go round in a consistent movement. It decides timely beginnings and a timely demise."

From a young age, Algar had known about the crystals. He'd use his power to mimic their different abilities. His fascination still sticks with him.

"The Water Crystal is said to be in an ancient temple on the island of Skantzoura, Greece. It's in the shape of an aquamarine and brings fresh water to human civilization. It's a key power in maintaining life. It provides for sea animals and commands all bodies of water and all liquid. Then there is the Earth Crystal. In the possession of the nomadic

African tribe of Nushoa. Known for their abilities drawn from the crystal. The jewel commands all minerals, rock, and soil on the surface—controls all wild animals. Prevent natural disasters such as earthquakes and volcanic eruptions from harming civilization. It also brings oil to the lands."

"What about the Moon Crystal?" asked Algar.

"The Moon Crystal contains the power of the Moon. It controls the tide and the night. It can summon unknown power from outer space. It also acts as a communication internally and to other worlds. Don't forget that. Finally, the most powerful crystal of them all is the Spirit Crystal. Currently possessed by the Indian Government and the sacred jewel of the Taj Mahal, Agra, India. The gem dictates life and death. Commands the personality and well-being of a person. The crystals' power is immense, and changes form. Many nickname it the Gem of Mischief."

"We've entered through the atmosphere."

"Brilliant. Open the ship's external door. It's time to start gaining." the being said as he jumped out of his ship.

Agent Carlson stepped up.

"For over 52 years, the Moon Crystal has been under our watch. It powers this facility and provides extraterrestrial intel. Five days ago, we received a message from the Moon Crystal. The encrypted code described an extraterrestrial spacecraft approaching the moon. Intel has described the ship as property of Gain of the Galaxy."

"What is Gain of the Galaxy?" Algar questioned. President Zalkon stepped up.

"Not a what, a who. Gain is from an unknown planet. Our research says he was born weak and without life. He travels from planet to planet, draining its life by gaining its life crystals. It's what keeps him alive and powerful."

"Prepare weapon 6-F23 and aim at the target." Gain said while floating in the sky above the facility.

"Yes, sir."
President Zalkon continued.
"This is your mission. You and Agent Carlson will work together. Gather each of the five crystals and bring them back here. Once you do that, we'll combine their power and place it into you temporarily. Before Gain makes his move on our planet."

"Fire on my command. 3..."

"You will use your power combined with that of the crystals to defeat Gain and save our planet from Gain once and for all."

"2...."

"Do you understand your mission?"

"Yes, sir. We won't fail." Algar declared.

"You can't."

"1...."

"It's time to begin work. This mission has to be done speedily. We mustn't give Gain time to prepare. Retrieve the crystals in this order: Moon, Time, Water, Earth, and Spirit. Travel accommodations have been set up. Go now and don't...

Suddenly a loud siren went off. ALERT! ALERT! This is not a drill! ALERT! ALERT! An unidentified flying being is in our airspace. ALERT! ALERT!

"FIRE!"

Agent Carlson sealed the door and engaged Intruder Protocol. The sound of a faint missile could be heard as it grew louder and louder. Then, an explosion shook the facility. The second explosion rang, cracking the stone structure. The third missile sound started faint. Then grew louder and louder and louder. Algar felt a quake in his powers.

"Take cover!" Algar exclaimed. The third missile was cataclysmic. The entire facility was reduced to rubble, along with some of the surrounding area. What used to be a sheltered underground sanctum became bare, and the sun could be seen from where the facility was.

Algar, covered in dirt and stone, woke up and rose to his feet. He saw Agent Carlson trapped under rubble. With his strength, he concentrated his power and cleared the rubble crushing Agent Carlson.

"Algar, what happened here? Where are the generals and the officers? Where is President Zalkon? Where is the Moon Crystal?" asked Agent Carlson.

They were nowhere to be seen. In the distance, Algar spotted a luminous being. Crystals of various colors rotate and form a ring behind him. The being is pale in color and sends shockwaves of evil down Algar's body.

"Gain." Agent Carlson said.

"Gain? That's him?" Algar asked.

Gain bent down slowly and rose with something in hand. Algar could feel the exposed power radiating from Gain's hand. It was the Moon Crystal. The power of the crystal flowed through Gain. The pupil of his eyes turned gray. He added the crystal to the ring behind him.

"Agent Carlson, stay low. I'll handle him." Algar said.
Gain looked around and spotted Algar. He called out.

"Are you human, custodian of the crystal?" Gain asked.

"I don't know where you're coming from, but stealing isn't allowed on this planet. You need to give me the crystal and leave." Algar said as he channeled his power to his palms.

Gain moved the crystal to his palm and stared at it.

"Very well. Let's see what this crystal can do." Gain declared.

Algar made the first move and began to fly toward Gain. Gain clenched the gem, and the sun darkened. A giant meteor was covering the sun, hurtling toward Algar.

"Ah, so that's what it can do." Gain said. Algar stood staring at the massive object in shock. Algar used his concentrated power and halted the meteor while pushing it back into outer space.

"Have fun with that. One down, four more to go." Gain said as he flew away. Algar drained his stamina but successfully saved the capital city and surrounding area from annihilation. Algar dropped to the ground in fatigue. He turned to Agent Carlson.

"What now?" he asked.

"The mission begins."

TIME

OVER THE PACIFIC OCEAN

Algar and Agent Carlson are flying over the Pacific Ocean in a United Governance airplane.

"There is a military outpost in Fukuoka, Japan. From there we move to Hong Kong by boat. Then to Chengdu by road." Agent Carlson said.
Algar was quietly seated. He was watching an international news broadcast.

Yesterday, catastrophe struck the United Governance of America. At about noon, in the Sayer Flatlands outside the capital city. An extraterrestrial being descended from the atmosphere wiping out an unknown underground facility holding the Moon

Crystal. 18 Major Generals and 22 high-ranked officials were killed in the attack. President Zalkon is in critical condition. As for the Moon crystal, witnesses say that it disappeared with the being. The world quakes at the attack and fortifies for the next.

"This is it," Algar said.

"What?" Agent Carlson asked.

"This begins the battle for our existence. Suppose Gain gets all five crystals. He'll drain all life from the planet. We know he'll get the gems in their ancient order. Moon, Time, Water, Earth, and Spirit. That's what we'll follow as well."

Algar stood up and moved to the cockpit.

"Pilot, how close are we?" he asked.

"40 miles from the Japanese Air Force Base." the pilot answered.

"There is a time limit. I am your assigned pilot. In two days at noon, I'll fly into Chengdu and fly out with you, Agent Carlson, and the crystal."

"Understood. May I get your name?" Algar asked.

"Agent Okeke," he answered.

After about five minutes, Agent Okeke announced,

"We are now descending on Fukuoka, Japan."

FUKUOKA, JAPAN

The plane landed. Agent Carlson and Algar stepped out onto Japanese soil.

"UGA Fukuoka Air Force Base, the largest base in Japan," Algar said.

"There's not much time to admire it. The ship is waiting on the other side of the base. This mission needs to be quick and efficient. One wrong move can decide the fate of our world." Agent Carlson replied.

They quickly moved into the ship. A team of colonels led them both on the ship to the War Room.

"Since Gain has taken the Moon gem, he needs to retrieve the Time Crystal next. Without the Moon Crystal, there's no telling where he is. That's why this mission needs to be done quickly. In about an hour, we'll dock in Hong Kong. Since the attack on the UGA, every nation has fortified its borders and the mainland. Especially China. You'll have to move with caution. Getting arrested isn't going to help our mission. Agent Yang here will move you to Chengdu by noon tomorrow. You'll have to locate Master Fang on your own. Since Gain has the Moon Crystal, it won't take him long to locate the Time Crystal. Retrieve the Time gem from Master Fang, and Agent Okeke will fly you to your next point."

"Understood." Algar agreed. Soon after, they docked in Hong Kong.

HONG KONG

Algar and Agent Carlson began their journey across China.

"Agent Yang, how long have you worked for the UGA?" Algar asked.

"Uh, about thirteen years."

"Really? What compelled you to join?"

"My family couldn't muster up money for college, so I joined the Marine Corps. I took a liking to it, and the government recognized my talents. I slowly rose the ranks and became a special agent based in the Pacific region."

"What about you, Agent Carlson? What brought you here." Algar turned to ask Agent Carlson.

"I've worked here for about 20 years. I was born into the Hagen family in Norway, one of the richest in the country. The responsibility and pressure threw me off the bar, and I ran away at the age of twelve. I was kidnapped and brought to America. I freed myself from captivity and fought off my kidnappers. When the police arrived at the scene, they took me to the Secretary of Defense.

Since that day, I became a special agent to the President and for every president since."

"Wow. That's incredible. I don't know what to say." Algar said.

"You guys should probably get some rest. Tomorrow's the big day." Agent Yang suggested. They went to sleep that night. The following day, they woke up in Chengdu.

CHENGDU, PEOPLE'S REPUBLIC OF CHINA

The following day Algar was woken by Agent Carlson.

"Up, up. We're here." Agent Carlson said. Algar slowly opened his eyes to see a large city with bustling life and energy. He imagined what it would look like if all of it were drained of life—bodies filling the streets.

"I can't believe something would want to destroy this all," Algar said.

"Well, not everyone has the privilege of natural life. More and more fill Gain's head. It clouds the judgment. The fear of losing his life torments him. The fear of death is that death cannot be altered. That's what makes the Spirit Crystal so powerful." Agent Yang said.
Agent Yang pulled over near a curb.

"This is the stop. Good luck with your mission,

agents." Agent Yang smiled.

"Thank you," Algar said.

"Agent Carlson." Agent Yang said.

Agent Carlson nodded. Then he drove away.

Algar and Agent Carlson scour the city looking for Master Fang. Their source says that he is located in the Wangjiaguai Residential District.

"We need to take a break. It'll be dark soon. Let's stop in this park here." Agent Carlson said.

Algar looked up at the sign to see 人民公园.

"People's Park." Agent Carlson read.

"You read Chinese?" Algar asked.

She looked at him and moved forward. Suddenly, Algar felt a chill in his spine. A powerful presence.

"Agent Carlson, I think I know where Master Fang is."

Agent Carlson turned toward Algar, and her eyes opened wide.

"Algar, turn around," she said.

Behind him was Master Fang.

"Come, quick." Master Fang said.

Yellowish energy engulfed his palms and he used it to carry them using his power. They quickly flew across the sky and landed in a small shop. Master Fang gestured them in.

"I know why you're here. You've come for the Time Crystal." Master Fang said.

"I won't give it to you. Gain already has the Moon Crystal. I wield the power to protect it; you don't."

"With all due respect, Master, the UGA chose me for this mission because of my rare abilities," Algar said.

"Then why couldn't you protect the Moon Crystal when Gain was right in front of you? You had the crystal first. He came and took it from right where you stood, yet he left with the gem, and you were empty-handed."

"You can't face Gain alone. You draw your power from the Time Crystal, like many others. You are the most powerful of them. If Gain takes the crystal from you, we will lose two battles already." Agent Carlson said.

"I see a future where I give you the crystal and Gain destroys all life on Earth." Master Fang said.

"Then we must fight. When two or three are gathered in unity, who can stop them?" Algar declared.

The light of the sun suddenly dimmed. Agent Carlson opened the shop door and went outside. The moon was large and full, and a being could be seen in the sky.

"He's here," said Agent Carlson.

An explosion shook the city. Master Fang and Algar ran outside to see Gain in the sky firing using his power upon the city. People began to run helter-skelter as fires roared and vehicles toppled.

"We need to act fast." Master Fang said.

"Sire, we've located the Time Crystal."

"I see it. It's coming right to me." Gain laughed. Master Fang was flying right to Gain. Algar and Agent Carlson tried to keep up. They could only watch.

"Custodian of the Time Crystal. Today shall be your fall." Gain decreed.

"我會用我的生命保護時間水晶" Master Fang exclaimed.

Gain replied, "Exactly."

Gain moved three crystals from his arsenal before him and fired three blasts toward the city. Master Fang revealed the Time Crystal, and the yellowish glow of power became red. A shimmering red gem appeared before Master Fang. The blasts were moved from this time. Algar and Agent Carlson watched the battle as Gain and Master Fang matched each other's abilities.

"What should we do?" Algar asked.

"You need to get up there. I'll help coordinate getting people away from this area." Agent Carlson said.

They agreed. Algar flew into the air.

The battle continued between Gain and Master Fang. Master Fang grew exhausted. Algar made it into the sky and joined the fight.

"Time Crystal custodian, do you grow weary?" Gain mocked.

"Master Fang, are you alright?" Algar asked. Master Fang was breathing heavily. Then a conviction hit him.

"Go," he said.

"What?" questioned Algar.

"Go now! Take the crystal. Get out of this city. You must survive with the crystal."

Algar took the gem. He felt a sudden rush of power. His eyes turned red as he used the crystal to enhance his speed. Gain wasn't happy.

"Oh no, you don't!" Gain exclaimed.

He moved a crystal before himself and created a spear from the power. He dashed after Algar, impaling Master Fang as he passed him. Master Fang dropped to the ground with a cloud of dust. Agent Carlson rushed after Master Fang. She found him dead.

Gain chases after Algar and the crystal as fast as he could. They zipped across the city, but Gain knew he wouldn't be able to catch up. An energy as black as night surged through Gain.

"Crystal thief, this move is how I destroy nations. Now, it will be how I destroy you." Gain declared.

Dark energy engulfed him, and Gain aimed for Algar. Algar knew what was to come and all he could do was brace himself. The power fired off in a dark stream. The beam just barely missed Algar. The sheer force knocked Algar off trajectory, dropping the Time Crystal while crashing into a cloth awning. Gain descended to the ground. Breathing heavily, he picks up the red jewel. Streams of red energy surge around him as he absorbs the power. He exhaled in delight.

"So this is the power of time on Earth. Hang on," he said.

"It seems a little full. Let's empty it."

He closed his eyes as red energy swirled around him. Algar was badly beaten and couldn't move. Gain opened his eyes which were now red. All the swirling energy left Gain and gathered in the sky as a large time portal. Then and there, everything Master Fang and all the previous crystal keepers sent to another realm of time descended onto the city.

"That ought to take care of this wretched city of misery. Soon all life on this putrid planet will belong to me, and its power will be mine."

The city was in ruins as fires roared and bodies filled the streets. Gain flew off, leaving it this way.

Agent Carlson ran to Algar, who lay defeated on the curb.

"Algar, what happened?" she stammered. "We blew it."

WATER

ATHENS, GREECE

"How is the Water Crystal?" the Secretary said.

"It's currently on its way here from Skantzoura Island, ma'am."

"Good. Get it here as fast as possible. Contact the prime minister and homeland defense. I need air support here fast. Begin the fortification of the city. Once the crystal gets here, lock everything down."

"Yes, ma'am. What about the people coming in from China?"

"Who?"

"The United Governance's agents fl ying in."

"Let them in when they arrive. However, do not surrender the crystal."

GAIN'S SHIP

"I'm almost there. Three more crystals, and that's it. But I fear that humans with abnormal power and abilities to wield and use the power of the crystals will delay my progress." Gain explains.

"Maybe you need to scramble their logistics, sire. "

"Maybe you're right. Maybe a distraction or a disadvantage."
Gain pondered for a moment but then came to a realization.

"Set coordinates as 27.997, -82.4553 and begin the descent."
The ship began its descent on Tampa.

TAMPA, UNITED GOVERNANCE

As people move about the busy Tampa streets, they see a giant dark spaceship appear from the clouds. People brought out their phones and began taking pictures and posting on their socials. Soon the ship ascended back into the clouds, and all that was left was a radiant pale man. His voice could be heard across the city saying,

"This world will soon be lifeless! With the power of time, I disable your privilege of more time!" The red jewel moved before Gain. Its glow became brighter. Every crystal forming the ring behind gain became a glow of red as spiraling energy engulfed him. On the surface, he was seen as a star the color of blood.

OVER AEGEAN SEA

Agent Carlson comes to see Algar in a blanket watching the news.

"You watch the news often, don't you, Algar?"

"Agent Carlson, look at this."
Algar points towards the television monitor.

This morning an unprecedented disaster struck the city of Tampa in the United Governance. A being now known as "Gain" descended in a spacecraft around 11 AM. The being exited and began to glow red so bright that it shone over the whole city. Every living thing in Tampa and the Tampa Bay area appears frozen in time. Along with all clocks, watches, timers, stopwatches, and every other machine or technology involving time in a 1000-mile radius. Nations believe Gain used the Time Crystal he stole from Chengdu, China, which he destroyed yesterday. More news to come.

"His power is growing stronger, and we're no closer to stopping him," Algar said to Agent Carlson in despair.

"No, we have. We are about ten minutes away from Greece. We got a message that the Greek government moved the crystal to Athens. Considering the current global situation, the three remaining crystals, Water, Earth, and Spirit, are under high security. Water's security is quite extreme."

Just then, Agent Okeke announced,

"Now beginning descent on Athens, Greece."

ATHENS, GREECE

Algar looked out the window of the plane. He didn't see a bustling town of life like Chengdu. There weren't any people on the streets like in Tampa. It was an expansive military base. Right in the center of the city was a large operations tower with a shimmer of blue light coming from the top window.

"There," Algar said.

"That's where the Water Crystal is."

Agent Carlson peered and agreed.

"That's where we're headed."

They landed and entered the operations facility. The defense secretary came up to Algar and Agent Carlson.

"Hello. Welcome to Greece; I'm sorry for the terrible circumstances," she said.

Algar greeted her and asked who she was.

"I am Defense Secretary Natalia Kalamos. I am overseeing the defense of the Water Crystal. I'm afraid we can't just hand it to you."

Algar sighed.

"Here we go," he murmured.

"Your failure to protect the Moon Crystal in the UGA Capital resulted in a meteor the size of Olympus Mons almost destroying your entire region. Your failure to protect the Time Crystal in Chengdu, China resulted in a time capsule emptying on the city, killing thousands."

Algar sighed again.

"Your excellency, we understand. We predicted as much. We are here to help defend the city. But, if somehow you don't give us the crystal and Gain rains fire on the city and the people, the blood is on your hands." Algar declared.

The secretary put on a disgusted face as she stormed off.

GAIN'S SHIP

Gain coughs and wheezes in distress. Heavily breathing in pain.

"Sire, please just relax. You've overexerted your power. The Time Crystal drained your life force. Don't exhaust yourself, or you'll run out of life energy."

"No. No. No," says Gain weakly.

"I must retrieve the Water Crystal. It will restore me to full power. But, I cannot go and get it myself. Knowing those humans, they've fortified since I wiped out that city and frozen most of a nation in time. Send in Ozo 3-F4H."

"Where, sir?"

"Set its coordinates to 37.937, 23.7729. Effective immediately."

"Yes, sire, What about you?"

"Set our coordinates to 9.765, 28.4096. I have a meeting."

Back in Athens, Algar, Agent Carlson, and the Greek Military prepare for battle. Algar contemplated to himself. He knew there was no way Gain would leave Athens without the crystal. He knew we would destroy the city. He thought about stealing the crystal and escaping, but that would result in a bound defense of the city, not the gem. Gain would wipe the whole peninsula off the map.

"Agent Carlson, how will we deal with Gain and trying to get the crystal?" Algar asked.

"I'm not so sure. All I know is that he'll be here any minute, and a total war will break loose."

The city of Athens remained still and quiet as they waited. After half an hour, a large cube-like ship darkened the city. Everyone looked up in shock. The secretary got to the control room.

"Fire ground to air missiles now!" she ordered.

Rounds of twenty ballistic missiles were fired every five seconds. The ship had a large force field protecting it, and each missile detonated on the force field, shaking the city. Algar had a bad feeling.

"Agent Carlson. We need to move."

"Where?" she asked.

"To the field. We need some kidnapper killers right about now."
Agent Carlson agreed, and they set off.

After five minutes of consistent but meaningless fire, the rounds of missiles stopped. The force field was disabled. Then the ship began to break into tens of tiny cubes. Tens turned into hundreds; hundreds turned into thousands. The ship was now like a cracked wasps hive.

"Air support, go now!" the secretary said.

A dozen teams of a dozen fighter jets zipped into the sky, launching smaller missiles and firing twelve magazines of bullets per second. Some bullets bounced off, but all the missiles took them out. Tens of these cube ships began to fall to the ground. Agent Carlson was puzzled.

"Why aren't they firing back?" she asked.

"It's part of their plan. They don't want the people. They want the crystal only. The fact that Gain didn't come himself is quite significant. He pleasures in human demise, but he sends these things for the gem alone." Algar replied.

"What does that mean?"

"He's running out of life."

Every cube began to intentionally drop to the surface until it was face to face with Greek soldiers.

"Charge!" the secretary commanded. Everyone charged forward, including Agent Carlson but not Algar.

"Algar, where are you going? The fight is this way."

"I need to get to the command room. I need to get the crystal, and we must get out of here. If we continue to stall Gain's progress, we can kill him without a fight."
They agreed, and Algar flew away.

The battle roared as soldiers fired on the cubes and the cubes fired back. Algar flew through the command room window.

"Secretary, we need to talk," Algar declared.

She had a nasty look of anger on her face. She left the room with Algar, and they walked down the halls of the Command Center.

"You need to give me the crystal. Gain gains power and life from the crystals he gains. That's why we call him Gain. Since the battle at Chengdu and the consecutive Time attack on the United Governance, he's drained his strength and grasp on life. We can keep it this way and defeat him without a fight. He can't touch another crystal without possessing it in the ancient order."

"Then why can't you just go for the Earth gem?" she asked.

"We also have to follow the ancient order. The Moon and Time crystals are already in Gain's grasp. If we go for the Earth crystal without first possessing the Water, the power of the crystal will drain our life." Algar replied.
The secretary thought for a moment and then sighed.

"Alright. Go and take the crystal. My only condition is that you use the crystal's power to destroy our current adversaries destroying our city." Algar agreed. He hurried back to the command room. He slowly approached the pedestal of the crystal and laid his right hand on it. The power surged through him. Blue energy churned around him, and his eyes glowed sapphire. With the crystal in hand, he soared out the window. From the surface, a blue fire was burning in the sky.

With the power swirling, he converted it to a whirlwind of water around him. With axillary strength, he gestured both arms toward the battle. Then and there, every cube turned into a pool of water as they dropped to the surface. The battle was won, and the crystal was in Algar's possession. That evening Agent Okeke flew into Athens.

"So, how did it go?" he asked.

"We did it. Let's quickly leave for the next crystal. Let's not let our luck run short." Agent Carlson said. And with that, the Water Crystal was safe from Gain, and the world revered the Greek Military.

EARTH

OVER WEST AFRICA

"Alright. The Nushoa are a nomadic tribe of powerful Earth Crystal-wielding Africans. They travel over all of Sub-Saharan Africa. Usually in West or Central Africa." Agent Carlson stated.

"So, where are we landing?" Algar asked.

"The United Governance has a base in Port Harcourt, Nigeria. From there, we'll search the region by hovercraft."

Algar agreed. Agent Okeke announced, "Now descending on Port Harcourt, Nigeria!"

At this point, they've heard those dozens of times, but for a purpose. Operation: Earth Crystal has begun.

PORT HARCOURT, NIGERIA

They landed at the UGA Base in Nigeria. They were greeted by a man named an agent.

"Welcome to the 5th Division UGA Base in Port Harcourt. I'm Agent Kenneth Nwosa, proctor of agent missions in North, West, and Central Africa."

"It's good to meet you, sir. We need to get to our hovercraft and begin this mission." Algar stated.

"Of course. Just right this way."
On the way to the hovercraft, Agent Nwosa gave them information on their mission.

"We got a tip that the Nushoa tribe is moving toward this region. You should meet them if you follow this route."
He then handed them a map. They entered the hovercraft and began to follow it.

The day turned into night pretty soon as Agent Carlson drove the craft. The ride was peaceful, and Algar sat in peace.

"Agent Carlson, is this your first time in Africa?" Algar asked curiously.

"No. I've been to Africa about twenty other times. I've been to Johannesburg and Capetown in South Africa. Along with Kano, Abuja, Port Harcourt, and Lagos in Nigeria. Addis Ababa, Algiers, Cairo, Accra, Yaoundé, Kinshasa, and about several other times." she responded.

"So you're a worldwide agent?"

"Yes, I've worked for the UGA in almost every country worldwide."

Suddenly there was a loud rumble from the earth. The craft had hit a large rock and toppled to the ground leaving the vessel in ruins. Agent Carlson crawled out of the craft's ruins to see a man glowing green before she passed out.

Algar jolted up, breathing heavily. He saw that he was in a bed in some sort of facility. A man walked into the room.

"Hello, Algar Newman of America. Welcome to Nushoa, the secret Earth Crystal Capital."

EARTH CRYSTAL CAPITAL

"So Nushoa is the capital's name, not the tribe!" Algar exclaimed in surprise.

He was walking with the man who had entered his room. He was the Chief of the Tribe and overseer, wielder, and protector of the Earth Crystal. Agent Carlson was with them too, but she wasn't as excited as Algar.

"We know your mission, Algar, and you've come to take the crystal. And it's yours." the chief said, much to Agent Carlson's surprise.

"Really, you'll give us the crystal just like that?" Agent Carlson said.

The chief smiled and nodded.

"We here in Nushoa would like to help you defeat the evil Gain. We can use the Water gem you've collected and the Earth jewel to defeat Gain."

"That sounds like a plan to me!" Algar said. Agent Carlson seemed troubled.

"Algar, could I speak to you for a minute?" she asked.

Algar agreed, and the chief walked ahead. He began to glow green and flew out of the hall and into a large open space with other tribespeople who were also flying with green energy. In the center of the open was the Earth Crystal in a metal containment which was powering every tribesperson.

"Don't you think this is all a little disarming?" Agent Carlson asked.

"Disarming? How?"

"Well, whenever our vessel crashed, I saw a glowing emerald being looking upon the wreck. And maybe the power of the Earth Crystal brought the craft down," she said.

Algar thought for a moment until the Chief

appeared behind him.

"You have nothing to worry about. You'll be fine here. Come, let's eat." he offered.

That evening the entire tribe sat at one large table with the Chief, Agent Carlson, and Algar seated at the head of the table.

The chief made an announcement.

"I now commence this feast in honor of Algar and the Water Crystal. They've graced us by being here tonight to help defeat Gain once and for all!" The people cheered in supposed excitement. Agent Carlson didn't eat. She sat there politely with deep trouble in her eyes.

After dinner, the Chief led Algar and Agent Carlson to a large room where they moved the Earth Crystal. Its power is shared across the tribe floating in its energy powering through the metal bars. There is an identical one right beside it but with no crystal.

"This is where you'll keep the Water Crystal to protect it." the Chief said.
Agent Carlson turned toward the Chief with her gun drawn.

"Agent Carlson, stop. Stand down!" shouted Algar.

"What are your true intentions? Who are you working for!" exclaimed Agent Carlson.

The Chief raised his hands in the air. They stood there for a moment in a stare-off. Then, the Chief gestured his finger forward and then toward himself. The Earth Crystal zipped toward him and entered his grasp. The power swirled around him, illuminating him and his eyes turned green.

"No!" Algar exclaimed.
The Chief grasped the gem, and the rock of the Earth built up on Agent Carlson and Algar, immobilizing them.

"You know, this could have been easier," said the Chief.
Then and there, his eyes turned gray.

"The Moon Crystal?" Algar said in shock.

"Gain," said Agent Carlson.

"In this flesh, yes," said Gain, who was speaking through the Chief.

"What did you do to this tribe!" Algar cried.

"A small spell. Nothing too major. Possessing their bodies and using their power to act like a battery to me directly. But thankfully, you fell for that. Hook, line, and sinker."

The Chief's body walked over to Algar and cleared a space in the rock holding him. He ripped the pocket and removed the Water Crystal. The power surged through and mixed with the Earth Crystal's power making a cyan color of energy.

"Ah, I can feel life returning to me!" Gain exclaimed.

"You can't win. You won't win!" Algar decreed.

"Oh. I already have."

Agent Carlson broke out of her captivity and fired multiple shots at the Chief. The power of the crystals deflected it. Gain fired a beam of power which she dodged and began to run toward him. She fired the finishing blow using her gun. The chief's body fell to the ground. It broke into pieces of rock which opened her eyes, and gray energy swirled. The energy manifested into flesh, and Gain's true form appeared. The pale skin and rotating crystals came back.

"Did you miss me?" Gain laughed.

Gain and Agent Carlson got into a battle while Algar was trying to break free. Gain had put Agent Carlson to the ground in a matter of seconds. She was out of the fight. Algar broke free and looked at Gain with vicious intent. Gain looked back. His pale pupils sent shockwaves down Algar's spirit.

"Now that I have both crystals. I don't need to entertain you, people."
His eyes turned green as the entire capital began to crack and crumble.

"From dust, you were made, and to dust, you

shall return." Gain laughed, and he vanished using the Moon Crystal's power.

The capital that Gain built for this attack crumbled into rubble from an earthquake Gain unleashed. Now that he has the Earth Crystal, the very ground on which humans live is at his command. Algar and Agent Carlson have to find a way. Somehow, to defeat Gain once and forever. No mistakes. No carelessness. They must get to Spirit, the most powerful of all, before Gain.

SPIRIT

SOMEWHERE IN CENTRAL AFRICA

Algar and Agent Carlson sit around a fire in a forest somewhere in Central Africa. They were slowly trying to make their way to a nearby city where they would contact the UGA in Port Harcourt. They only had three days until they died of dehydration. Algar carried Agent Carlson for hours flying around looking for a city until he grew tired. On day two, they found nothing. On day three, they looked and walked the whole day. They grew hopeless until they heard noises of civilization. They moved faster and faster until they arrived in the city of Wau in South Sudan.

WAU, SOUTH SUDAN

They moved around the city looking for some way of communication. The suburb area was tightly compact, but eventually, they found a telephone booth. They needed to hurry. Gain could already have the Spirit crystal for all they knew. Algar had confidence, though. He knew the previous battle took a lot out of Gain, and he needed to recuperate even with the Water and Earth Crystals. The telephone rang.

"Hello, this is United Air Base Port Harcourt." the operator said.

"Little House on the Prairie." Agent Carlson said.

Algar was confused. What was she doing? he thought. There was a three-second period of silence.

"Welcome, Agent Carlson."

Algar's eyes widened in surprise.

"I'm requesting a lift from my current location due to an accident in my mission." Agent Carlson said.

"Downloading your geographic coordinates. Coordinates 7.7092° N, 27.9835° E have been downloaded and approved. Lift arriving in fifteen minutes."

The operator then hung up. Twenty-three

minutes went by, and they were still waiting. At the twenty-five-minute mark, a jet created a whirlwind of dust as it landed in the middle of the town. Agent Okeke poked his head from the door.

"I haven't been to South Sudan before, but of course, it's because of you two," he said jokingly.

"Ten minutes late isn't a joke," Algar said with a chuckling grin.

"South Sudan isn't Nigeria now, is it? Come on, hop in! You have serious work to do, seeing that you ended up here."

OVER THE ARABIAN SEA

"This time, we can't just barge into a battle. We have to have a strategy, a defeating-blow technique." Agent Carlson suggested.

"You're right; what would that be?" Algar pondered. Then he had an idea.

"Gain inflicted catastrophic damage to cities and peoples all over the world, right?" Algar started.

"Right." Agent Carlson replied.

"How?" Algar asked.

"Using the power of the crystals."

"Yes. That also drains his life force, right?" asked Algar.

"Correct."

"The Crystals' powers are being discovered new all the time. We only know the basic things they can do for certain. The Spirit Crystal is one of the most mysterious. Gain has studied these jewels and knows what they can do. If he gets his hands on the Spirit Crystal, his life force will be off the charts due to the large concentration of power in one gem."

"He'll be unstoppable." Agent Carlson said.

"Right, but what if we drain his power while defending the crystal all the same?" Algar suggested.

"How?" she asked.

He replied, "When we land in Agra, we aren't going to deal with the protectors of the Spirit Crystal. Shah Jahan adored his vast jewelry, and his most prized possession was the Koh-I-Noor, said to be given to the British Monarchy. It was buried with him in the Taj Mahal. I need you to sneak into the Taj Mahal, retrieve the Spirit Crystal, and bring it to me. Its level of power can match that of the other four crystals unified. By then, Gain will have descended in power and strength. During that time, you need to coordinate the evacuation of the city and nearby towns and villages. My power and the power of the crystal will conjoin and create a dome forcefield to trap me and Gain within it. I know I may not be able to defeat Gain, but our match in strength and energy will hold me long enough for all his might to drain. When Gain collapses in exhaustion, I'll take the crystals and obliterate his soul, defeating him once and for all."

Agent Carlson looked at him for a moment. She then smiled.

"Excellent plan, Agent Newman."

AGRA, INDIA

The final mission was on. They landed in Agra and immediately went their separate ways. Agent Carlson headed for the Taj Mahal. Algar went to the rendezvous point. There was a large crowd outside the Taj Mahal, but no one could enter. Guards surrounded the ivory-white mausoleum.

"Here we go." Agent Carlson said to herself.

She moved through the crowd to the front. She gently reached for her non-lethal weapon. She moved to the right side of the Taj Mahal. She had to act fast. Gain could already be on his way. The sides were less guarded. She broke through the barricade as the few guards scattered in confusion. Easily enough, she entered the Taj Mahal to the chamber in which the tomb of Shah Jahan sat. There were three guards in the chamber room. Agent Carlson reached into her pocket and pulled out a small device which she threw into the room. It released a paralytic noise, making the guards drop to the ground like flies. She carefully moved into the room, closer and closer toward the tombs. A top of one of them was a large white diamond encased in marble.

"Bingo," she said.

She pulled a pair of pliers out and forcefully removed the Spirit Crystal from its containment. The marble cracked, and the gem was released. Its power surged, and rouge energy spun around the room. Agent Carlson carefully placed it inside a metal cube to contain it for the trip to Algar. And like that, the Spirit Crystal was acquired.

Agent Carlson began to rush toward the rendezvous point. She knew she had taken too long. But, she made it to Algar in time.

"Here's the crystal," she started as she handed him the metal cube.

"I'll begin the evacuation of the city. And Algar,"

"Yes?" he responded.

"Don't lose."

She then raced away on her bike.

Algar opened the cube and revealed the powerful jewel. He gently reached in and pulled out the gem holding it in his hand.

"Hm. This isn't so bad," he said to himself. Just then, the power raced through Algar's body. He screamed pure pain as the Spirit Crystal dealt with him. The searing energy faded and tamed itself. Algar was breathing heavily. He heard a laugh like that of a child coming from the gem.

"I guess that's why they call it the Gem of Mischief," he said. He focused his power, and blue energy rushed into the gem from Algar's fingertips. This now put the crystal under his command. Algar was now as powerful as Gain himself. Algar, with his new enhanced abilities, jolted to the sky in a split second and released four sky blue energy concentrations toward the surface. This was in preparation for the dome force field. Algar knew Gain was on his way. He was ready, and so was the world.

Suddenly, a large meteor entered the atmosphere, hurtling toward the city. Algar bolted to the surface of the meteor, and with one powerful push, he expunged it out of the atmosphere and back into space. Gain was here.

A gray portal opened in the sky, and Gain descended from it. Algar could see him levitating in the sky with him. He had a scepter with a multi-colored glow in the jewel at the head. The colors were as listed, gray, red, green, and blue.

"You combined the power of the crystals!" Algar exclaimed.

"Yes, but I see that you possess the Spirit Crystal's power along with your own." Gain replied.

"You don't have to worry. Your destiny ends here." Algar decreed.

Gain looked at Algar with a grin. Then, the jewel of the scepter shone bright blue. Algar was surrounded by small ice needles.

"Don't get destiny confused, human. It's yours that ends right now!"

Algar then extended his arms, enacting a large dome force-field around Algar and Gain.

"Now, you can't summon gigantic meteors. Your powers don't work outside the dome." Algar said.

"But they do inside!" Gain exclaimed as he gestured a fist toward Algar.

All the ice shards began to hurtle toward Algar. He created a protective sphere around himself until all the shards were gone. The staff shone red as a time portal opened, summoning the same needles back toward Algar. This time he flew upward as a sky blue energy manifested in his palms. Several sky blue power arms materialized swords in each hand behind Algar, and they zipped toward Gain. "I just need to hold him long enough to drain his energy," Algar said to himself. Before the arms could reach him, Gain disappeared.

"What!?" Algar said.

He began to search the dome as his heart beat faster and faster. Algar could feel his presence. Behind him opened up a gray portal as Gain slowly crept out of its scepter in hand. The head of the staff materialized into a spear tip which he drove through Algar. Algar shrieked in pain.
Gain grinned.

"You see! You have failed!" Gain exclaimed. Algar's head began to turn slowly. When his eyes were visible by Gain, they were white. Gain gasped and withdrew the scepter from him, but it wouldn't budge.

"Excellent." said a voice.

"What is this!?" Gain was puzzled.
Algar appeared on his right-hand side. The fake Algar grabbed the head of the scepter and smashed it to pieces releasing the jewels. Gain was now freed, and in urgency, he picked up three of the fallen crystals. The fake Algar picked up only one and rushed back to the real one.

"Is this what you're looking for?" Algar asked. He held up the Time Crystal for Gain to see. Gain was furious. He placed the three crystals on his chest, and an energy armor engulfed and protected

Gain.

"It's over for you, human!"
Algar did the same as Gain with the Spirit Crystal and Time Crystal.

"I notice that you're growing slightly weaker. Let's finish this!" Algar exclaimed.

Gain summoned three smaller meteors from inside the dome. It can't get too large, or else it would destroy him as well. He hurtled them toward Algar. Algar began to fly toward Gain, blasting through each meteor. Then a red glow engulfed each piece of debris and reversed them back into three meteors launching back at Gain. Gain yells in anger as he rips them apart using the Moon gem. From his chest, each crystal glows as he launches a beam of all their power. In an attempt to match the power, Algar does the same. The powers collided, creating a light show so bright that it lit the whole city. Algar's power began to prevail as Gain's weakened. Algar's power blasted Gain to the wall of the dome, and Gain crashed to the floor. Algar began to glow red as the Time Crystal enhanced his speed. He zipped toward Gain and ripped another crystal off his chest. Gain pushed him away as he stood up. All Gain now has was the Water and Earth Crystals.
Gain cried out in a fury.

"You can't defeat me! So stop trying!" Gain yelled.

"Your powers are diminished. It's only a matter of minutes before you exhaust your life." Algar replied. Suddenly Algar was out of breath and gasping.

"Don't you think the crystals are exhausting you too? Don't be fooled, human. My power is still better than yours!"

Gain began to glow green as large rock spikes came from the ground toward Algar. Everywhere Algar moved, spikes stopped him. His power extended into an arm and picked a large spike, hurtling it toward Gain. Gain gestured a glowing green fist toward the incoming spike, breaking apart. He then created a large hole in the ground below Algar. Magma erupted from the ground up to Algar. He shielded himself in a protective sphere when Gain appeared within the sphere. He drew out a sword of ice. Algar defended himself with his bare hands. Struggling with Gain, he began to grow weak. But so was Gain. To break Algar's hold, Gain glowed blue, and water began filling the sphere. Gain ejected from it, and so did Algar.

"You're running low on choices. Luckily for me, I still have many!" Gain said.

"I need to activate my final move, fast. But

I need all the Crystals of Existence." Algar said to himself.

Gain began to gasp and was breathing heavily. Clinging to his breath, he began to glow green and blue. Ice and stone shards filled the dome. Gain collapsed on his knee, breathing unremittingly. All the shards fell to the ground.

"This is my chance!" Algar stated. He soared toward Gain and grasped him by the neck. That wasn't a way to kill him, and he knew his plan.

"You aren't strong enough to defeat me." Gain said weakly.

"Oh, but I am. You're the one who's too weak." Algar stated.

He pulled off the Water Crystal and then the Earth. He blasted Gain to the other side of the dome. He carefully placed the last two crystals with the others on his chest. He began to glow with the surging power. Algar's power linked all the crystals together. Gain on the other side of the dome, stumbled to his feet.

"You now possess all the crystals and have the chance to eternal life, yet, you chose to save this planet of humans. Are your meaningless lives blind to death!" Gain exclaimed weakly.

"I don't fear death the way you do. You fear

death because you know that it can't be altered. And now you face it." Algar said.

Each crystal began to glow brighter and brighter. Gain began to glow as well, screeching in agony as he faded away. And like that, Gain was defeated forever. Everything and everyone he destroyed, killed, or froze was restored. They had fought the good fight. The battle was won.

RETURN

Algar and Agent Carlson returned to the UGA Capital and were welcomed with a parade that lined the streets. They met with the fully restored to health, President Zalkon.

"Congratulations, both of you. For a job well done. I trust that every crystal was returned where it was found and that the world is now safe." Zalkon stated.

Algar agreed.

"Yes, sir. The world can now rest with confidence that they are safe. And if any threat returns, we'll be there."

And with that, the crystals continued to bring

prosperity to the Earth.

ABOUT THE AUTHOR

Ephraim Nwabuko is twelve years old as of writing this book. Along with being an author of fiction and realistic fictional stories, he plays the cello. He loves watching different shows and movies and uses what he's seen and read to create new book ideas. Born and raised in Texas, he loves to travel, discover new experiences, and channel what he knows through writing different stories and characters.